TAKE ME TO YOUR LEADER!

poems by

Richard Stevenson

Illustrated by Joseph Anderson

  Bayeux Arts

Take me to your leader
Richard Stevenson
Joseph Anderson
© 2003 by Bayeux Arts

Published by:
Bayeux Arts Incorporated
119 Stratton Crescent S.W.
Calgary, Alberta, Canada T3H 1T7

Printed and bound in Canada

The publisher gratefully acknowledges the assistance of the Alberta Foundation for the Arts, the Canada Council for the Arts, and the Government of Canada through the Book Publishing Industry Development Program.

National Library of Canada Cataloguing in Publication

Stevenson, Richard, 1952-
　　　Take me to your leader/Richard Stevenson; Illustrations by Joseph Anderson

Poems.
ISBN 1-896209-86-6

　　　I. Anderson, Joseph, 1973- II. Title.

PS8587.T479T35 2003　　　　jC811'.54　　　　C2003-905356-3

These poems are for Adrian and Marika,
their friends and classmates.
May the thunder of their hooves,
their raucous laughter
continue to grace our home.

Acknowledgments

Some of these poems have previously appeared in *Alternate Realities, Canadian Author, The Crosstime Journal, Dark Moon Rising, Dream Forge, Freefall, Ibn Qirtaiba, Lethbridge Living, On Spec, Outer Rim,* and *Power Animal*; others have been accepted for the chapbook Spaced Out (Midnight Star Publications) and the anthologies *The Canadian Anthology of Modern Verse For Children* and *Tesseracts*[7]. Thanks to the editors for their support and encouragement. "Aliens In The Freezer" appeared in my previous collection, *Why Were All The Werewolves Men?* (Thistledown Press, 1994). I reproduce it here because of its obvious thematic connection to this manuscript of new poems. Thanks to Paddy O' Rourke and the fine folks at Thistledown Press for their support of my work.

Thanks to Dave Merriman for setting "Cattle Rustlers From the Skies" to music, and helping me get the poem published as a song in *On Spec*; and to my other musician friends and accompanists Peter and Ryan Heseltine, Don Ponoch, Dana Beauchemin, Murray Nelson, Alex Thompson, and Gordon Leigh, for their improvisational skills and talent, which made various public performances and rehearsals of some of these poems so much fun. You've been great, guys; may we all get into the studio again down the road apiece and record some of these pieces.

Finally, a big thank you to my wife, Gepke, and my children, Adrian and Marika, for listening to the various drafts and offering their sage opinions. Thanks for the title too, Gep!

CONTENTS

1. SILLY SEASON

II. ALIENS IN THE FREEZER

III. ANGEL HAIR

IV. BLACK HELICOPTERS

I. SILLY SEASON

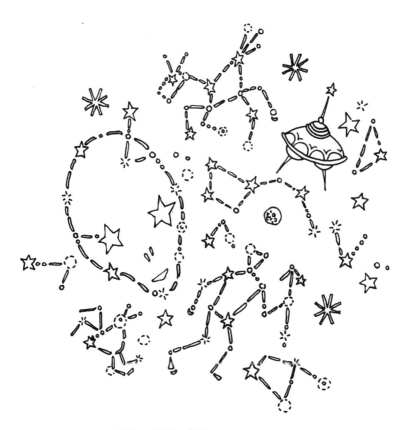

The Big Dipper

When I was just a little guy
I'd look way up into the sky
and try to count the stars out there
while standing in my underwear.

I could not see the crab or bull,
and wondered: with the sky so full,
who decided to join the dots that way
to make these pictures anyway?

I'd make my own pictures then, of course –
join this star to that and make a horse,
but what I really wanted to see
was a flying saucer, just for me.

I look at the heavens with wonder still:
see the Big Dipper about to fill.

Silly Season

Get out your cameras and videocams!
Grab your binos, load up your vans!
The sky is a switchboard of traveling lights!
It's time for saucers and marvelous sights!

It's silly season! Reporters take note:
Bigfoot will boogie; bodies will float
outside their windows on blue tractor beams.
Nothing will ever be quite what it seems!

Grinning green men will walk through your walls,
MIBs ask dumb questions in shopping malls,
sea serpents will flash olive green coils,
boys will be boys and go after goils.

If you've got a dog, better go call 'er.
Abominable swamp slobs are down in the holler.
You ain't got time to watch the news:
Chupucabra's slaverin' after your ewes.

Time to hobnob with goblins down in the glen,
grab cheap seats in saucers with little green men.
Mothman's back with his fiery red eyes.
Ain't nothin' like the element of surprise.

The Nazca Lines, the Great Pyramid,
the subtle subconscious and dithering id,
the great grey wastes of the unconfined
are hanging out vacancy signs for the mind.

Punch my ticket! Beam me up, Scotty!
The government scoffs; the leaders are dotty.
Spaceship earth's wobblin' off course.
I'll try my luck with grey intercourse.

If there ain't no room in the A 'LE' INN,
book me a room less high falutin'.
Somewhere in the outer meninges will do.
I'm tired of humans. How about you?

Foo Fighters

"Where there's foo, there's fire,"
'toon hero Smokey Stovel said,
and the next thing we knew
foo fighters were flying overhead.

Ball lightning, reflections off ice,
according to nay-saying aces;
but antic, intelligently directed,
they put our pilots through their paces;

rode shotgun at their wing tips,
did pirouettes, zig zags, and flips;
appeared, disappeared in a wink.

We'd squint, rub our eyes, and blink.
Say St. Almos' fire does not dance,
and maintain our stalwart trance.

The Greys 1

Well, I was drivin' home one night
when somethin' tol' me to turn right,
and I know it sounds absurd,
but it weren't no voice I heard.

It's like I took a notion
to jump into the ocean:
I drove through open fields,
eyes glazed as that windshield's.

I drove back roads through the tulies,
over hills and dales and coulees,
'til there weren't nowhere to go,
and I saw this bluish glow.

Well, I got out of my truck
(I was bogged down in the muck)
took my shank's mare up a hill
like some zombie with no will.

Next thing I know it's dawn;
I wake up on my lawn.
The truck's parked beside the curb.
Who's grinnin' at me but Herb.

Have some java, Jack, he says,
like some mad monkey in a fez,
and I'm a sousled organ grinder
who lost his arse and couldn' find 'er —

only I weren't out on no bender,
didn' so much as dent a fender.
Still, it was off to see the shrink
to find a program for folks who think.

The ol' lady she looked at me
like I was a bucket a pee.
Said, Next time you dive in the roses,
please spare me the nekked poses.

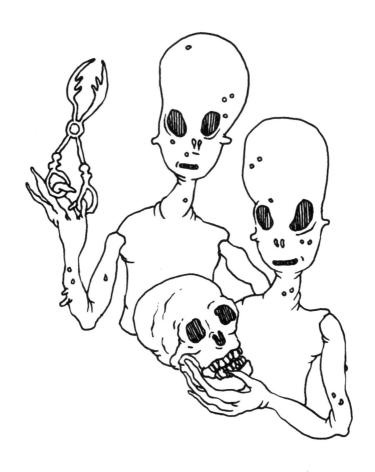

Well, I saw me a hypnotist
to see if he could gimme the gist
a what had happened in bluish light
in that farmer's field that night.

He said, Count to a hundred and three
and I'll tap your memory.
Don't worry about nothin' at all,
cos I'm here to catch your fall.

So I shifted my butt 'n' drifted,
and, you know, he's awful gifted;
I muttered some stuff and screamed
and he told me what I dreamed.

Well, I dreamed I saw a saucer
and I very nearly tossed 'er,
when some bug-eyed little guys
stared deep into my eyes

and, with telepathic powers,
and pleasant misty showers,
they calmed my ruffled feathers,
undid my clamps and tethers,

said what I found myself aboard
weren't no Japanese Accord
or secret Russian rig
on some high-tech spyin' gig.

I wasn't travellin' incognito
with some badass space bandito,
or sittin' high in the saddle,
about to space skeddaddle.

I was on some interdimensional ship
and they wanted to make me hip
to the comin' apocalypse —
only — I swear — they got no lips!

They told me (by telepathy— no guff —)
about the future of our species 'n' stuff —
how they've been monitoring me
since I was two or three;

how we've stressed this here planet
with every Jackass Jess 'n' Janet
to ever pollute a stream
or hatch a housing scheme.

Said they're greys,
got shy 'n' retirin' ways;
don't like our brutish manners,
gonna keep us on their scanners.

Gonna snip a little tissue,
improve our minds and issue,
grow in vitrio hybrid golem,
grey-human whatchamacallem

and colonize new stars
from Andromeda to Mars,
prevent we silly peoples
from raising bomb-shell steeples.

Well, I tol' ol' Marge the story;
she said, That tale's hoary —
got more hair on 'er than your head.
Best not tell ol' ramrod Ed.

Now Ed's the sheriff here,
and he's seen stuff that's queer,
but nuthin' the like a these greys
with their telemetrickster ways.

So I have said nothin' for years,
'cept what I've just clapped to your ears,
so I'd appreciate your silence too,
'til they come some day for you.

You'll know 'em when they arrive,
and find out this ain't no jive.
They'll walk right through your wall —
little grey guys four feet tall.

They got those deep black mantis eyes
that somehow talk and hypnotize,
long skinny fingers, grey clammy skin.
You'll go stiff as a mannequin.

You'll try to scream, of course,
but you won't. They don't need force.
They'll just teleport you on beams,
then nothin'll be what it seems.

They'll examine your every pore
'til you're a puddle of fear on the floor,
then you'll wake up in your bed
with a faint buzzing in your head.

Nothing will be the same again.
Not the sun, not the wind, not the rain.
They take your molecules apart,
and that is just the start!

The world's a curtain a matter
they part like some mad hatter.
They'll come frequently for you too,
and there's nothin' — nothin' you can do.

The Greys II

Well, we got shy, retirin' ways.
You know we wear no green berets
because we got no flag to raise
and we don't need no reveilles
because we're fey, inscrutable greys.

Yeah, we don't drive no Chevrolets,
don't need no paved highways,
don't write no roundelays,
don't keep no résumés
because we're fey, inscrutable greys.

We don't eat no fish fillets,
don't slurp no consommés,
don't sip cafe au laits,
don't need no fresh ashtrays
because we're fey, inscrutable greys.

We don't eat no canapés,
or flans or fresh frappés
or petite dejeuners;
don't cherchez or sashay
because we're fey, inscrutable greys.

We don't send no attachés,
or wire communiqués,
or wear real hair toupées;
got no blazé or fatuous ways
because we're fey, inscrutable greys.

We don't need no airstrips or runways;
we land where cattle graze,
would rather milk the milky ways
than shovel glacés or purées
because we're fey, inscrutable greys.

We don't need no sweet parfaits,
don't respond to bold bouquets,
didn't come here pour parlays,
ain't no hab habitués
because we're fey, inscrutable greys.

Ain't substantial anyway.
There's nothing to assay
or photograph or portray;
our half-life on this half-tray
is about to decay...

because we're fey, inscrutable greys.
Halloween hobgoblin greys.
mantis-eyed, egg-headed greys.
Saucer telemetrist greys.
Going, going, gone greys.

Good Sci Fi

With so many ideas drifting by,
why don't they make more good sci fi?
There's always an alien plot, it seems,
to invade the earth or someone's dreams.

Buildings are blown to smithereens
while politicians scheme in alternate scenes
how best to kick the aliens' butts
or outsmart some superior bionic putz.

Like the bully in the sandbox who gets his
after kicking and smashing all our toys,
the aliens kick our military behinds,
when along comes Test Tube and the boys.

Wouldn't it be great, if, once, instead,
geek aliens met humans with big foreheads?

There's a Fungus Among Us!

There's a fungus among us
that comes from outer space!
It's not terribly humongous –
just a smidgen, just a trace.

It came back on a space probe
on fuselage and wings.
Only showed up under strobe
as fluorescent dusty rings.

We thought it was corrosion
from our atmosphere,
metal fatigue, erosion –
certainly nothing we should fear.

It didn't look alive, at first.
What could live in empty space,
in a vacuum we'd traversed?
It didn't seem so out of place.

Looked like regular wear and tear –
gamma ray pitting or friction
from abrasives in our air –
not something outta science fiction!

But then one cell became two,
and two became four.
We didn't know what to do,
what this fungus had in store.

We couldn't break down a gene,
discover the DNA code.
Nothing on the cellular scene
was so perfectly bestowed.

Now the fungus differs from what it was!
It's got a ghoulish patina,
is a glowing, pulsating fuzz!
Someone recite a new novena.

Pray we contain its growth!
Our scientists are stumped,
have been sworn to a secret oath;
the military is pumped!

They don't know what it is,
but maintain official wraps.
It's bubbling acidic fizz
is dissolving all their traps!

X-rays cannot kill it.
Heat just slows it down.
It's like a monstrous teenage zit,
a microscopic acne town!

What if its putrid pustules pop
and spread insidious spores?
Who knows what spray will stop
or keep these spores indoors?

This ain't a sprinkle of moon dust –
we're talking creeping chartreuse ooze!
There ain't no one to trust.
Our species might just lose!

So far, the military assures us,
they've got the crisis in hand.
While a new fungus may be among us,
no contagion's spread or planned.

They say the stain's contained.
Everything is controlled.
Then why are the gates still chained,
why is the base so well patrolled?

Why mum's the word or death?
Why the blackout on media news?
Why am I speaking under my breath?
What is it we stand to lose?

Maybe it's worse than Ebola or AIDS!
Maybe it grows like a fuzz on our brains!
Maybe it's broken the barricades!
Maybe it's claimed new earth domains!

There's a fungus among us, for sure!
A nasty microscopic stain.
It's hardier than the soup du jour.
Its one thought: how to remain!

It doesn't need much to survive –
a few grey cells, a little skin.
Its spores hitch-hiked a ride.
Now it's thicker than original sin!

There's a fungus among us.
It's gonna grow on everything!
There's a fungus among us!
It's gonna leave a ring!

There's a fungus among us!
Lord, God, hear our prayers!
There's a fungus among us!
It's caught us unawares!

Ain't no fun, Gus – please hold!
It's worse than total fission.
Ain't no mildew or mold:
it's a mother with a mission!

Yeah, there's a fungus among us.
Ain't no fun, Gus, I'm told.
There's a fungus among us,
and it's really taken hold!

It's gonna spread around the globe!
It's gonna gobble up the grass!
It's gonna grow on every lobe,
every wrinkle and crevasse

of every fold of grey matter
to hold a thought intact.
Gonna flow, and grow, and spatter.
I tell you it's a fact!

It's here! The situation's clear!
It's gonna live and breed among us.
Gonna multiply and persevere.
It's gonna be humongous!

A humongous fungus among us…
a giant hungry spongy tongue
of bumbling, fumbling, encumberous
glutinous, mutinous, mucous mung!

There's a fungus among us!

The Sky Is Cryin´

(with apologies to Elmore James)

The sky is cryin';
look at the tears roll down the street.
The sky is cryin';
look at the tears roll down the street.

I been lookin' for my baby.
I wonder, where can she be?
I'm lookin' for my baby.
I wonder where can she be?

Saucer folks done took her,
whisked her into space.
Saucer folks done took her,
whisked her into space.

Came through the walls and nabbed her
while she was wide awake.
Came through the walls and nabbed her
before she could cook my steak.

Now the dog and I are moanin',
starin' at our empty plates.
The dog and I are moanin',
starin' at our empty plates.

Gonna have to get used to rare, I guess
or switch to boiled tube steaks.
Gonna have to get used to rare, I guess
or switch to boiled tube steaks.

Gonna turn the stereo on,
listen to a little mo' Elmo' James.
Gonna turn the stereo on,
listen to a little mo' Elmo' James.

Ol' Blue he'll howl at the moon.
Guess I'll accompany him some.
Ol' Blue he'll howl at the moon.
Guess I'll accompany him some.

And we'll learn to like our cookin'
before our days are done.
Yeah, we'll learn to like our cookin'
before our days are done.

Maybe greys make better husbands:
don't want no washin' done.
Maybe greys make better husbands:
don't want no washin' done.

Bin two years in these long johns;
guess it's time to scrape 'em off.
Bin two years in these long johns;
guess it's time to scrape 'em off.

Dog's plannin' on leavin' too it seems:
ain't fleas enough for two.
Dog's plannin' on leavin' too it seems:
ain't fleas enough for two.

Ain't no saucer gal to beam me up.
Gotta stick it on the farm.
Ain't no saucer gal to beam me up.
Done used up all my charm.

Pwdre Ser (Star Jelly)

Heads up, guys!
Watch yer noggin, John!
It's fallin' from the skies!
It's goopin' up yer lawn!

Star jelly! Star jelly!
Ain't no glue or paste.
Star jelly! Star jelly!
Ain't no known waste!

It's flyin' saucer lube goo!
Putrid purple slime!
Gelatinous residue!
It's droppin' all the time

Star jelly! Star jelly!
Fishy vichyssoise!
Star jelly! Star jelly!
Got no human cause!

Don't get it on yer skin,
or in your hair or eyes.
You don't know where it's been;
it turns off worms 'n' flies!

Star jelly! Star jelly!
Gobs are bein' dumped.
Star jelly! Star jelly!
Scientists are stumped.

Maggots cannot hack it,
bacteria vamoose;
no virus will attack it,
sure don't smell like mousse.

Star jelly! Star jelly!
Creeping chartreuse ooze.
Star jelly! Star jelly!
Got some on my shoes.

Now my shoes are movin'
all by dem 'mazin' selves.
They're dancin' 'n' a groovin'
with others on the shelves.

Star jelly! Star jelly!
That's some wicked slime!
Star jelly! Star jelly!
The stuff is keepin' time!

My shoes got hot foot blues;
they're infected with the beat
of flyin' saucer lube ooze
and unseen stinky feet.

Star jelly! Star jelly!
What am I gonna do?
Star jelly! Star jelly!
I haven't got a clue!

I caught some in a jar,
the jar began to bop;
I got out my guitar,
and, you know, it couldn't stop.

Star jelly! Star jelly!
I think this stuff's alive.
Star jelly! Star jelly!
Sure can shuck and jive!

I tried to slow it down
by playin' it a dirge;
it got down on the groun',
began to burp and surge.

Star jelly! Star jelly!
Ain't no earthly blob.
Star jelly! Star jelly!
It soon began to throb.

I tried some jazz and funk,
some R & B and soul;
it glommed into a hunk
of black and shiny coal.

Star jelly! Star jelly!
Man this stuff is weird!
Star jelly! Star jelly!
I'm afraid it's what I feared.

The stuff is pure willpower
devoid of self and sense.
It grows bigger by the hour
and glows it's so intense.

Star jelly! Star jelly!
Gimme some a dat.
Star jelly! Star jelly!
I'm gettin way too fat.

I spread some on my belly,
put a dab behind my ears.
Now I sell it on the telly
and it's conquered all my fears.

Star jelly! Star jelly!
it'll make your spirit bounce.
Star jelly! Star Jelly!
I sell it by the ounce.

Now I'm drivin' a Mercedes
and livin' on the hill.
I'm pop'lar with the ladies
'n' have a patent on the pill.

Star jelly! Star jelly!
Yeah! That's my bread and butter.
Star jelly! Star jelly!
Get to sit around and putter.

Now you can have yer goose grease,
your prunes and Spanish fly;
gimme a condo in Nice
and some jelly from the sky.

Star jelly! Star jelly!
Plugs every orifice.
Star jelly! Star jelly!
Fills my soul with bliss.

The Oz Factor

How is it these E.T. guys
can zip down silently from the skies
right over the shuck-and-jive
of traffic roarin' down I-5 –
midday, midnight, any time –
and no one notices them arrive?

I tell you, it's high strangeness, man –
the Oz factor. I'm in my van,
just motorin' along, when, suddenly,
for no reason I can see,
I get the notion to change lanes –
things start to get real strange.

I take an exit to Nowhere, it seems –
call it Nod, the land of dreams,
or maybe it's the real twilight zone;
I'm thinking, " Woah! Hold the phone!
I've just come off an underpass.
Where's the traffic? I'm out of gas?"

My car sputters, craps out anyway.
Then I'm sittin' next to a field of hay!?
They've turned off my headlights.
Got rid of the smog and urban blight.
Hell, I can't hear a frog or bird,
let alone a discouraging word!

Man, talk about travellin' incognito!
These guys don't just mess with my magneto;
they come with a portable reality,
a Loonie Tune wormhole patch, maybe.
Like Bugs, they lay it down just so,
and down their rabbit hole you go!

Only I'm Elmer Fudd, hot to trot;
Bug's reached up and grabbed the spot.
I'm left stammerin' the usual refrain:
Did this happen here or in my brain?
Of course I've got no evidence,
and that puts me squarely on a fence.

Is this some kinda cosmic joke?
I dunno, Doc. Where's the cloak?
Is some Porky Pig alien gonna poke
his head out of the credits yoke
and stutter, " Th-th-th-that's all, folks"?
Is this all some kinda mental hoax?

35

Or am I the quazzy wabbit here?
The situation is doggone weird.
I just can't click my heels thrice,
though Kansas is startin' to look real nice.
Send me anywhere in space and time.
Tie up loose ends, make 'em rhyme?

Show me how to grab this spot,
fold it up, stick it in my pocket, Doc.
You know I can't believe my senses.
Nothing's solid. No farm or fences.
The hair between my ears is growing,
but, baby, there ain't nothing showing!

Puttin' me in a rubber room
won't get me out of this cartoon.
I ain't light in my loafers, Dad,
but I need ruby slippers bad!
This Ozzy/Loonie Tune universe
is goofier than rhymin' verse!

II. ALIENS IN THE FREEZER

Hey There, Little Grey Guy

Hey there, little grey guy
with deep dark mantis eyes,
I really dig you, baby,
but you caught me by surprise.

Your saucer's somethin' else, man,
trés chic and very cool!
I'd like to take a spin with you,
or maybe just a tool –

around the farther planets
to Zeta Reticuli,
but I gotta do my homework
and I'm too young to die.

Yeah. Space is so capacious —
I really like to fly –
but I gotta do my homework
and I'm too young to die.

We can trip the light fantastic,
stop by The Milky Way,
have cocktails at a Mars bar
on any other day,

but now I'm in my jammies,
got curlers in my hair;
have to clip my toenails –
I can't go nowhere!

You know I like to levitate –
anti-gravity's a gas!
I'd love to beam up with you, babe,
but tonight I gotta pass.

Yeah. Space is so capacious,
I really like to fly,
but I gotta do my homework
and I'm too young to die.

I love your bedside manner, babe –
the way you float down halls.
You're so quiet and considerate
when you walk through walls.

You don't have to ask me anything:
you just read my mind!
A guy with so much forehead
is really hard to find.

You're a wizard with obstetrics,
my laser leprechaun;
free my thoughts of so much dross
with your oh-so-special wand;

and space is so capacious,
I really like to fly,
but I gotta do my homework
and I'm too young to die.

Aliens in the Freezer

Ask Doctor Gee if you don't believe me.
They're little perfect people
with little perfect teeth;
they have no known diseases;
and eight-toed hands and feet.

Gee told Newton; Newton told me.
Saucer crashed out in the pass;
Air Force nabbed and bagged em.
Seriously. Two little corpses
in a lab in a freezer
hidden away from you and me.

The winter of '48 it was —
in a big electric storm.
One o' the worst; sky nearly burst.
Saucer goofed on its co-ordinates;
the air force got there first.

A cover-up, a total scam —
every nut and bolt and fragment
of the saucer wreck inspected
swept up sorted and kept
for future reference.

Stored in a secret lab
in the desert
out west
where the only pests
are skeeters, kiyoots,
ranchers, rattlers
and addled-pated
tale tattlers.

Men in black suits,
black glasses
and boots,
old prospectors
so deranged
they ride the radio
-active range.

Travis Walton's Tale

You think I'm just some doofus
with a tabloid tale to tell,
some hick kid from the sticks
whose brain ain't working well.

You found a tabloid in the truck,
say I read some saucer story –
"Elvis Spotted on Saturn's Moon,"
or something just as hoary.

So now you've got me wired up,
take my pulse and make me sweat.
You're gonna prove I'm lyin',
show the world I'm all wet.

But I ain't lyin' Sheriff,
though, sometimes, I wish I was.
They got me with this tractor beam,
and my head began to buzz.

I must have blacked out then,
'cause the next thing I recall
is a mushroom smell, a mist,
and a long gray steel hall.

I was being hauled off to a lab
for some medical test or other.
They strapped me to a table.
I cried out for my mother!

They sprayed this wicked stuff on me
that turned into a shrink-wrap skin.
It clung like Cling Wrap to me,
held me stiff as a mannequin.

I was suffocating! They cut
slits for my mouth and nose.
They cut holes for both my eyes,
came at me with a rubber hose!

I was freaking scared! Couldn't move!
They nipped and poked and pried,
stuck this needle up my nose!
I smelled something that smelled fried!

My brain! It must have been my brain!
They were drilling … I could hear the whir,
feel the crunch of bone give way.
They inserted something – I'm sure!

Do you think I'd stick a B.B.
up my own nose for heaven's sake?!
I'm telling you: I saw them!
I was numb but wide awake!

That little spot on the X-ray –
it's a radio tag, I bet.
They're tracking us all like deer.
We haven't got the foggiest yet!

You can laugh your fool head off,
put me in a rubber room,
deny the evidence of your senses,
assume whatever you want to assume.

I'm telling you I was abducted!
I'm telling you we're bugs in their jars!
I'm telling you they're extraterrestrials!
I'm telling you they come from the stars!

You can tell me that I'm dreaming.
You can tell me that I'm nuts.
You can tell me that I'm scheming.
You can call me bionic putz.

It won't matter to them when they come.
It won't matter to them when they leave.
It won't matter if you decline the ride.
Sooner or later you're gonna believe!

Invasion of the Chupus

If you think all aliens are nice,
that they come here to watch over us,
then I better burst your bubble
cos the water's gotten muddy, Gus.

The reptoid species and greys
may abduct yer yankee boys
to do lab tests and impress 'em
with their hi-tech probes 'n' toys,

but down here in the hills of Brazil,
a jungle away from pryin' eyes,
they got some wicked badass ways
that ain't about us gettin' wise.

Folks in this no horse burg are poor;
they ain't seen no fat cat in a Cadillac,
let alone intergalactic saucer folk
who wanna give their heads a whack.

They spend nights in hammocks in the trees,
waitin' for dinner on the hoof;
they got no time to speculate
or gawk at the skies for proof;

but what they've seen, if they're
lucky enough to tell the tale,
scares the purple jesus out of them —
don't make them hearty or hale.

They call 'em chupus, silent deadly
flyin' refrigerators with microwave rays.
They got no windows, just two lights,
but manage to zap 'em anyways.

The attack is always the same, it seems.
They come in low, just over the trees –
bright stars, so bright they burn your eyes.
Don't make a sound, not a riffle or a breeze.

Suddenly, you can't move a muscle to leave;
you can only close or turn your eyes away.
They've spotted you, pinned you like a bug,
then a shaft stabs out, a deadly ray.

Hits you in the neck or chest – always.
Never in the extremities – a leg or arm.
Afterward, you feel weak, can hardly walk –
and they say aliens mean us no harm!

Dizziness and headaches follow.
Anemia, with low hemoglobin count.
No nausea or diarrhea – maybe.
Worse symptoms start to mount.

Red burn marks then turn black,
with two puncture marks inside.
Your skin turns deathly white.
Your hair falls out! You're terrified!

If you're lucky, you get to die!
But don't pay these "accidents" any mind –
No. The E.T.s are just overzealous –
they don't mean to hurt mankind.

Tell that to the poor peasant farmer
whose skin fell away from his bones –
microwaved or evenly roasted.
Hear his terrible throes and groans.

Are you gonna tell me I'm mistaken?
These E.T.s are really nice boys?
They just got something new for Christmas
and wanna try out their microwave toys?

Or maybe they're just winnowin' the race
the way we thin a garden row –
are givin' a few of us more space
so we can grow and grow and grow.

Brazil's so populous out here, of course –
if you count the mosquitoes and gnats,
and there are just too many insects,
and way too many bats!

They're killin' us with kindness, of course.
Practicing good animal husbandry habits.
Their humanoid stocks have surpassed
those of our cattle and rabbits.

We cannot ever get to the stars
when we're bumbling and fumbling about.
We're too busy climbin' our dung hills
to turn the Beagle hard about.

Mothman!

You may think I'm just a nut,
some hooped hippy all hopped up
on some hallucinogenic drug or other,
but let me tell you something, brother.

My hair is long, but I am straight.
My girlfriend and I were on a date.
We were just parkin' beneath the stars
a little way off from the other cars.

All the kids come here to neck,
and we did too, but, what the heck,
they don't call this place Point Pleasant
'cos folks come here to hunt for pheasant.

Besides, there were plenty of crewcut Pongos,
and they weren't smokin' or playin' bongos —
talk to some of them good ol' boys
with gun racks mounted in their toys.

They saw the same seven foot freak,
and it wasn't no crane sans legs or beak!
Do I look like some backwoods rube
or Trekie geek with Rubik's cube?

You think I just dropped off the back
of some turnip truck with haversack?
I've lived in Virginia all my life,
had just asked my girl to be my wife.

We weren't up to anything illegal,
and neither was Barney, my pet beagle.
So when he started to whimper and whine,
I know he wasn't protestin' no parkin' fine.

We shushed the dog, came up for air,
thought maybe he had smelled a bear.
Then a series of high-pitched bleeps
broke into static and station sweeps.

Much to my surprise, it proved futile
to try to get rid of 'em with the dial;
but we'd heard reports the night before
of oddities explained by a meteor.

So we thought we'd check it out,
get out of the car and walk about.
That's when we saw the mothman first —
and I thought that we were liverwurst.

It didn't look like no moth I've seen —
some reporter just got it in his bean
to name the beast after some brute
in a Batman comic, or somethin' cute.

But it was no laughin' matter, Jack.
Soon as I saw it, I thought: here's my back —
I'm outta here, only I couldn't move!
Hey! I ain't macho; I've got nothin' to prove!

It's just — well, you had to see its eyes —
fierce, piercing — We were hypnotized!
Hearts in our throats big as camel humps,
our hair on end — we were all goosebumps!

Then it let out a high-pitched shriek —
a heavily amped bat-like squeak.
I ain't talkin' deer mouse with a megaphone:
I mean piercin' to molecules of bone!

The thing had huge, bat-like wings —
I don't care what song the paper sings —
and no head! It's eyes sat in its shoulders!
And the fear they instill? Man, it smolders!

I felt like those eyes were laser beams,
and we were toast! Only now it seems
the thing might have let us be, if Barney
hadn't a felt his chili con carne.

Man, that dog lit into that cursed beast
like it was the critter lookin' to feast —
only the mothman scooped him up and flew away,
and we haven't seen Barney to this day.

It was the way it flew that freaked us out:
straight up — without flap of wings or a shout.
No war cry — not a sound. No huffing,
no puffing. Even from its wings, no luffing.

I can't explain it any better than that.
it was huge, but agile as a cat,
and when it flew, it soared like an eagle,
and absconded with my favorite beagle.

Did it ravage it into bite-size pieces?
Rend it from limb to limb to feed its nieces?
I dunno. All I can say is its hands and feet
were human-like and it was fleet.

It clocked our car at one hundred miles per,
screamin' eeeek! and was covered in fur.
And as for parkin' at the old TNT dump,
I ain't stupid, and my wife's no chump.

We stick to the outdoor drive-ins now,
and when we look at burgers, think brown cow.
I don't ever want to see those evil eyes,
but you bet I watch the darkened skies.

Pascagoula Creatures

Well, we're Pascagoula Creatures;
we got no eyes or features.
Where you good ol' boys got noses
we got stubby carrot hoses;
where you got those flappy ears
we got pointy carrot spears.
We don't need no brows or peepers:
we got radar-programmed beepers.
We wrinkly-skinned rhinocers
gonna float out of our saucers,
gonna beep beep beep our way
across this moonlit bay.
Gonna nab and bag you boys;
ain't gonna give you a choice.
Gonna take you 'board our craft,
while you stare gawk-eyed and daft.
Gonna nip and probe and pry
with a long snake through the eye,
collect some human tissue,
'fore we hypnotise and issue
a few post-hypnotic orders
'bout your crossing mental borders.
Then we'll set you back to fishin'
and you can go on wishin'
you catch your limit of dolly varden
while we beg your leave and pardon
and you stare at your ol' bobbers
and forget us space hobnobbers.
Ain't no point in fanning coals
of paranoid space goals:
you had yourselves a dream
'bout some interstellar scheme.
There ain't no Pascagoula Creatures,
'cept in Friday Creature Features.
Go home and watch your Raiders;
we ain't no space invaders.

Flatwoods Monster

Well, I'm the Flatwoods Monster, baby!
Oh yeah! Ain't no nos or maybe.
When I set down in my saucer,
you're gonna retch and toss 'er.

'Scuse my sulfurous salutation
that precedes my reputation.
That cloud on which I'm floatin'
ain't got no floral coatin'.

It's that hydrogen sulfide glide
that provides a cushioned ride,
though they don't call me the breeze
when folks fall to their knees.

Ain't really ten feet tall:
I just got no legs is all.
Since I ain't no damask rose,
it's good I got no nose.

But maybe it ain't my smell
that consigns me to your Hell.
Maybe it's my fiery eyes
that strike fear and hypnotize.

Maybe it's my monkish robes
that so inflame your lobes.
My black ace-of-spades collar
that makes you hoot and holler.

Ain't no space hobgoblin though.
The fireworks are just for show.
Got no Draculish intention –
or fiendish incisors to mention.

Pardon the lack of aplomb.
I just thought I'd drop a bomb –
float by on a little flatus.
Must you always hate us?

Loveland Frog

Well, you catch me in your headlights
on some lonely mountain road,
think I'm just some lonely coyote
or hobo with heavy load.

I get up off my haunches
and hop the roadside rail.
That's when you get a gander
of my tidy tadpole tail.

Yeah, my skin's all viscous, baby,
and glistens with moon glow.
My feet are webbed and flipperish.
I'm amphibious, you know.

Got uggy buggy frog eyes
and droopish triple chin.
Gimme high-five on the fly, babe,
and I'll slip you my cool fin.

For I'm the Loveland Frog, babe.
Got no croaky callin' card.
Gotta slip off to the bog now.
Yeah, don't you take it hard.

My grin is wide and Tupper tight.
Hey, dig these phosphor eyes.
Sorry I left my tux at home,
but you caught me by surprise.

Yeah, my skin's all viscous, baby,
and glistens with moon glow.
My feet are webbed and flipperish.
I'm amphibious, you know.

I got here in a saucer.
Your swamps are such a gas.
I'd really like to stay and gab,
but I'm afraid I gotta pass.

Yeah, I'm a five-foot-five bipedal guy,
and I really like to swim.
I'd like to do the frug with you,
and – ooo – I'm trim and slim.

We could slip between the reeds, babe,
get down and skinny dip.
You know I'm slippery when wet –
ain't jivin'! No, I'm hip!

Yeah, my skin's all viscous, baby,
and glistens with moon glow,
but I gotta do the time warp.
Babe, you know I gotta go.

My home is in the Pleides.
I'm a long way from my bog.
Ain't no glistening log, babe.
Call me the Loveland Frog.

Next time I'm through this wormhole
I'll hop by your pad, for sure,
cos my skin's all viscous, baby,
and you know my heart is pure.

Manimals

Hey, hey, baby, what's wrong wit chew?
Find somethin' hairy, gotta stick it in a zoo.
You know we furry hominids
didn' get chew in dis mess;
we jes sloggin' through the bayou,
doan mean you no distress.

Yeah, we jus takin' a vacation
in dis fetid funky swamp,
diggin' on the weeds
and compin' on a stomp.

We're manimals. (Argghh, manimals.)
Ye-ah, m-m-manimals.
Alabama boogers, abominable swamp slobs
(A.S.S. for short.)
Jus want to scratch our behinds,
bang on these hollow logs.

We tub-thumpin' hairy hipsters
limin' in limelight.
Our eyes are luminescent
so we can see at night.

Got three fingers. (Got three toes.)
Ain't no five-digit Bigfoot, baby;
(Ain't no local denizen.)
We're manimals. (Argghh, manimals.)
Boppin' in our saucers
from swamp to fen to bog.

Alabama boogers, abominable swamp slobs
slappin' skeeters on our bellies
while you feed yo' ugly faces,
gawk at monsters on your tellies.

Yeah, we're attracted to
that big pseudopod of blue
that has you fuzzy and depleted
the longer you stay seated.

You see us in your windows
and throw a hairy fit.
Jes cos we not clean-shaven
don't mean we am not hip.

But y'all dive for yer shotguns,
fill our hairy butts with lead
instead of maybe compin'
with our fetid stomp instead.

Oh yeah, baby, we're manimals.
(Hairy healthy hominids).
Ye-ah, m-m-manimals.
(Bigfoot saucer folk).

You got us in yer gunsights
(Want new pigs in your poke).
Hairy heathy hominids.
(Bigfoot saucer folk).

El Chupacabras
(The Goatsucker)

Well, down in Puerto Rico
where the sun shines high and bright,
they say a ghastly creature's
got the government uptight.

Its grabbin' goats and headlines.
Suckin' blood 'n' slime;
its drainin' stoats and rabbits,
nabbin' poultry 'n' prime time.

Oh, Chew-chew chu-pa-ca-bra,
you quill pig kanga-ra-too.
you're a vampire most macabre,
a real red-eyed nosferatu.

Chew-Chew chu-pa-ca-bra.
You wallaby wannabe,
you got yourself a mohawk,
now you're on a killing spree.

(Do Wop Chorus)

Chew chew chew,
Chu Chu-pa-ca-bra.
Gonna nab nab nab
a new ewe 'n' skedaddle.

Gonna suck suck suck
suck its succulence.
Gonna hop hop hop
over any wall or fence.

We draw your picture for the paper
but when we draw a bead,
you drop a dirty stink bomb,
our eyes... they almost bleed!

Your fiery eyes can hypnotize,
your wicked farts just wreak!
You grab a sheep, go on the lam;
we cannot move or speak.

Chew-chew chu-pa-ca-bra,
you ain't known to palaver –
leave the nasty callin' card
of a vampire or cadaver.

Chew-chew chu-pa-ca-bra
from whose coffin did you crawl?
Did you catch a flying saucer,
Were you ever here at all?

(Repeat Chorus)

They say you ain't no giant,
sport fangs like some ol' snake;
but you sho' don't stop to rattle,
and you doan clean up yo' plate.

Are you on a liquid diet, man?
You sho' love dem sanguine shakes
You leave bodies flat as wineskins
Are you sure you won't eat steaks?

A goat is a just goatskin, eh?
cows are just fat coats;
you leave their fur containers
like quaffed vanilla floats.

The blood runs thick and slow,
as ice cream down a glass.
Your wipe your lips, lick fingertips,
drop the empties in the grass.

(Repeat Chorus)

Hopkinsville Goblins

Well, we're Hopkinsville Goblins,
got hopalong ways.
Got here in saucers,
gonna land in your maize.

We've got big floppy ears
cos we're curious imps,
stare through your windows
like grinning green chimps.

We mean you no harm —
we're no bother at all;
still, you shoot out the glass
and blast through the wall.

Hit us with high velocity lead,
knock us lil fellers end over end.
You'd think we were robbers,
you had Fort Knox to defend.

Just cos we got big bulbous eyes
and talon-like meathooks
to pick, poke, and pry
doesn't mean we're alien crooks.

So put away the blunderbus, Gus,
hang fire with the thunderstick, Ed,
or we'll have to stop dancin'
and show off our toys instead.

Our silver lame body suits
may look like tin cans on your fence,
but you good ol' Kentucky boys
have no cause and no defence.

We tiny saucer goblin tricksters
could levitate your entire clan
out of your tawdry clapboard house,
into our double-pie saucer pan.

We ain't talkin' pie in the sky
coolin' on the windowsill, folks,
so give the school boy prank a rest,
stop pelting us with lead egg yolks.

Cattle Rustlers From The Skies

Well, we're cattle mutilators,
new body fabricators;
got homunculus intentions
and a whole mess of inventions.

Gonna zoom down from the skies
for some parts to hybridize;
zap some lone cow chewin' cud,
jack 'er up and drain 'er blood.

Gonna excise a few organs,
leave cleaner cuts than Dr. Morgan's;
leave that wide-eyed bovine corpse
and vamoose through space/time warps.

Chorus: Yeah, we're alien cattle rustlers,
              nasty high tech space abductors;
              gonna 'buse your dogs and horses,
              confound all yo' po-lice forces.

We're intelligent and devious,
presumptuous and ingenious;
ain't no way to stop us —
can't shoot or stab or bop us.

We're too advanced to catch.
Ain't no troops you can dispatch
to corral us cattle rustlers:
we're transient space hustlers.

Don't get your knickers in a twist or panic:
you know we ain't satanic;
we just need a hybrid golem,
a zombie whatyoumightcallem —

some genetic engineered body
that breathes air and ain't so cloddy,
so we can colonize your planet
and hang with any Ken or Janet.

Is Bigfoot an Alien?

Is Bigfoot a m-menancing
m-monster outa space,
or just a hairy old Houdini
who don't get in yo' face?

Is Bigfoot an audacious
saucey saucer kinda guy,
a chew-chew-chew Chewbaca,
or is he just a little shy?

Is Bigfoot a tremendous
teleported hunka spunk,
or just a hirsute doofus
who digs that swampy funk?

Could Bigfoot be an alien,
an outer-space outcast,
a trippy Giganto hippie
with a passport from our past?

Could Bigfoot be an alien?
I really want to know.
He always seems to turn up
to catch the saucer show.

Could Bigfoot be an alien?
That might explain his place.
A hominid hobgoblin?
Spaced-out specimen from space?

Could Bigfoot be a tourist
from galaxies away
who wound out of a wormhole
and wound up here one day?

Could Bigfoot be an alien?
Can the past occur right now?
Are there worlds inside of worlds?
How un-now brown un-cow?

III. ANGEL HAIR

Crop Circles

Call a ufologist! Gimme a cereologist!
I got circles in my barley! I got circles in my lawn!
My dog is going bonkers! My cat's hoop city too!
The frogs have all stopped chirpin'. My wife is really gone!

Wasn't no plasma vortex or dust devil here!
The patterns are too crisp, too complicated, man!
Show me a force of nature writing hieroglyphs!
We're talkin' Leonardo, some UFO Cezanne!

Look! It'd take six men six days to create
a design like this elaborate key shape here.
That polygon is perfect. No hoaxer could make
such subtle glyphs, not even an engineer.

How would he get here without leaving a mark?
There are no footprints; I'd've heard a chopper.
The grain is all laid flat, in a perfect whorl.
Not a stalk is broken. Put that in your hopper!

Whatever did this did it in the dead of night,
and did it undetected, without wakin' Rex!
I'd've seen lights. They would need a canon spot!
The designs, I tell you, the designs are too complex.

No. We're lookin' at deliberate language here.
These are symbols, some kinda cryptograms.
The E.T.s are sayin' they're among us.
They're sending galactic telegrams.

I bet they're pictures – models of some molecules,
or maybe mathematic fractal holograms –
something our scientists haven't deciphered yet,
but need to soon. Maps or wiring diagrams.... .

Schematics or hieroglyphics – maybe something ancient –
a language pre-dating the Egyptian's –
an antediluvian or Atlantan Christmas card,
or some such bizarre transcription.

Call Scotland Yard! Gimme the F.B.I.!
Send a cryptologist to break this cyber code.
We wanna set our best minds to work out here.
It's important, not just some graffiti goad.

None of the barley's damaged. None of the heads are dead.
Maybe they're telling us to look inside
to sow the seeds we need to sow.
The millennium is here. Our history's at high tide!

These ain't intergalactic doodles on some cereal pad.
We just don't get it yet. They're saying, "Yo!
Pick up the phone! Is anyone home here
on this third stone from the sun? Hello? Hello?"

Angel Hair

What is this fibrous, spindly stuff
that starts as vapor in the sky
and gathers in flocculent coils
visible to the naked eye?

Spidery tendrils of silly string
hang like harp strings in the trees,
but when I catch some in a jar
I might as well bottle the breeze!

The fibers plum disappear!
No snap, crackle, or poof,
or change to aqueous state;
no goop, no residue as proof!

It's like them saucer boys
were winkin' when they passed.
They dropped a load of bunting
cos they knew it wouldn't last.

Yeah. They did this wicked fly by –
put the Snow Bird boys to shame.
Flew loop the loop in tandem,
gooped my laundry just the same.

First, there's nothin' to see –
no vapor trail or hint.
There's no rumble of thunder,
just the saucer's silver glint.

I might not a spied 'em
If I didn't suddenly decide
to look up at the sky,
and I'd still be stupefied.

As it is, I'm befuddled by this stuff.
What it is has got me stumped,
though I swear I saw it forming
and know how it was dumped.

Is it some kinda space spaghetti?
Variable Wormhole vermicelli?
Reconstituted TV wave linguini?
Or fetid fallout from the telly?

Folks here call it angel hair,
but, I dunno; I can't see
a flock of angels losin' their locks
in shock over some saucer spree.

Nosiree. It's gotta be some strange
electro-magnetic force, some way
the greys have of warpin' time
or space. Wormhole castings, I'd say.

Ezekiel's Wheel

Did Ezekiel have a close encounter
of the fourth – or any – kind?
Or was this funky Ol' Testament prophet
just a geezer out of his mind?

Were the four wheels he saw in the sky
really saucers with E.B.E.s inside?
Did they beam the ol' guy up
and take him for a cosmic ride?

Or did God just drop the whammy,
put our ol' boy in a trance?
Was it God or the E.T.s that taught us
how to tell the dancer from the dance?

Ol' Nebachadnezer II –
let's call him Neb for short –
nabbed three loads of Hebrew slaves
and, as kings go, was of the nasty sort.

Ol' Zeke was force-marched to Babylon;
he didn't catch the fire of no reggae song.
He lived among the exiles in ancient Tel Abib –
We're talkin' 593 B.C. when the E.T.s came along.

They rode a cloud in heavenly chariots
to hear ol' Zeke frame up the tale –
but, hey, what else could he call 'em
when the craziest ride was in a whale?

He said those E.T. boys had wings,
wore one-piece lamé suits
(Well, we all know that all that glitters isn't gold,
and that, compared to them, we're brutes).

Now maybe they really beamed up –
kinda rose on invisible wings.
These gnarly Ol' Testament guys
wouldn't have known these things.

The dude he saw at his console
looked like a king on his throne,
so Zeke prostrated himself in awe
when he saw a cellular phone.

The E.T.s musta called Dispatch
before booting into hyperdrive,
for, when they dropped off poor ol' Zeke,
it took him a week just to arrive.

The E.T.s must have implanted
some transmitter in his gourd
cos he took the high road after that
and began mutterin' about the Lord.

They say he was a prophet,
this funky grey-beard loon;
I say they gave him a retrofit,
dropped him off on some sand dune.

Ezekiel's wheels got baby moons
and cruise the galaxy now.
They've got new chips, do time flips,
but still can't raise our brows.

Alien Implant Blues

Oww Oww Oww Oww Oww-www!
You know I've got a horrible headache, baby.
I'm in pain now ever-y day.

Can't seem to shake it, baby.
Ohhh, it's a mean m-m-m mother
that just will not go away.

Can't hear myself think –
It don't help when I drink –
Ain't no potion or pill I can take.

Yeah. I got the alien implant
can't-listen-to-the-boob-tube-
without-getting-the-Venusian-news blues.

You know I tried Feverfew,
Aspirin and Tylenol too.
Gobbled Anacin down by the pound.

I put Tiger Balm on my palm,
rubbed my temples and brow.
Don't know what I gotta do now.

Cos I got those mean ol' low down
squinty permanent frown
alien-bead-up-the-schnozzola blues.

You know my wife went out shoppin'.
I was on the phone talkin',
just gawkin' out at the sky.

Saw a strange reddish light,
just thought that I might
take a gander from the front porch.

Well, I got zapped by a beam,
smacked the back of my bean,
and blacked out for an hour or three.

73

Shrink hypnotized me.
That's when I started to see
these grey guys strappin' me down.

They had a drill up my nose,
a wicked will to impose,
a black bead to implant in my brain.

So, doc, won't you please
check when I sneeze,
get some long tongs and just op-er-ate.

My nose is a faucet,
and you know that I've lost it,
can't stand any mo' of this pain.

I got no will of my own.
It's like an alien phone
is permanently clapped to my skull.

They know what I'm thinkin',
can't seem to stop blinkin',
got the alien implant blues.

Yeah, they know what I'm thinkin',
I'm thinkin' of sinkin'
My po' alien brain down the drain.

Yeah gonna do the deep six
if I don't get outta this fix
gonna drown myself in the bay.

So help me, doc, please,
I'm down on my knees,
get this implant outta my brain.

Yeah. Help me doc, please,
I'm down on my knees.
Can't stand any mo' of this pain.

Life On Mars?

Who pulled the plug on Phobos I?
What glitch obstructed Phobos II?
Did Viking get too close to Mars
and break some space taboo?

Does some Great Galactic Ghoul
sit with laser on his knee
and pick off our tin cans
when they pass his vacinity?

That long shadow on the planet
in the last photo that was sent –
was that some Pac Man saucer
or last will and testament?

When Viking flew past Cydonia
it saw a human face.
Was that sphinx our Giza's sister
staring back at us from space?

Or were we, for the first time
in ten thousand years,
staring at ourselves that day
in a cosmic mirror?

Did E.T.s build the pyramids
on both Earth and Mars?
Did they build two lion sphinxes
and let us think that one was ours?

Were they shepherding the human race,
helping us make better toys,
so we could share the sandbox
and learn to play with E.T. boys?

Were we the little golems
they fashioned out of clay,
so we could learn to walk erect
and conquer space one day?

Were Adam and Eve an experiment –
just E.T. Barbie dolls?
Are we half ape and half E.T.,
a new species that paints walls?

Did we festoon our caves with images
that led to speaking parts?
Or are we just Chatty Cathies
with science strings and arts?

Eons ago did Mars look just like Earth?
Was there an Eden, did rivers course
through trees and valleys there?
Was the garden destroyed by some cosmic force?

Maybe we're Model 2, New and Improved
homo sapiens sapiens of some Eden 2 –
are mucking up our mucked out stalls
on some intergalactic zoo.

The E.T.s are back to tend their flocks
from bases beneath the sea,
or else they're busy little Frankensteins
hard at work on model 3.

Alien Autopsy Film

Ain't no kwashiokor kid
with stick limbs and pot belly,
no hollow-eyed, o-mouth invalid
or famine victim from the telly.

Ain't no progeria case
with translucent skin and melon,
big head and wasted face
some relief agency is sellin'.

Ain't no hairless monkey,
no crispy cosmonaut;
they say she smells too funky
for a latex movie prop.

Maybe she is our saucer sister –
some interstellar Stella
who crashed her rig. I dunno, mister –
but she sure ain't no fella.

They ain't stuffed her in no potter's field
in an unmarked box now, have they?
She's here in the all together, unconcealed.
What are they weighin' her brain for anyway?

Sure don't look like no brain I ever saw.
And what about those organs there?
Safeway giblets? That sticks in my craw.
Her insides are different; they don't compare …

Who would pony up the dough
for the convincin' rubber chicken
if this is a pig blood bladder show
made to make our pulses quicken?

Look! Blood weeps from each incision
of the doc's sharp scalpel blade.
He moves with a doctor's precision.
Yeah, the close-ups sometimes fade –

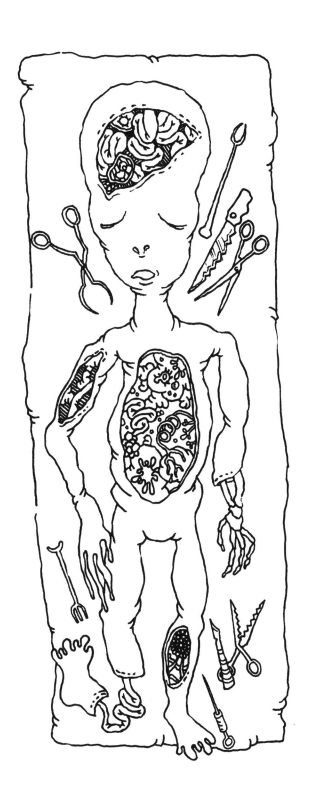

but they say that's old technology –
proof the cameras do not lie!
And there is no obvious anomaly
to the kind of phone or props nearby...

They say the film is forties stock –
it's got the maker's mark!
If all this footage is a crock,
it's an expensive lark.

If this ain't archival footage here,
someone took some awful pains –
for no money or fame? It seems clear
these ain't no mutant human remains.

Government woulda iced the guy
who sold this footage then.
Even now he's probably sly,
thinks folks'll cry fake again.

They called the Roswell crash
a weather balloon. He knows they'll lie,
say this footage is cheap video trash.
He's sly I tell you. Really really sly.

No. I'd say she's an E.B.E.—
alien from conk to toes.
Yep. Got an E.T. pedigree –
but from where, who knows?

Who Put the Bop in the Bop Shu Wop?

What happened to the Neanderthals
that got us lurkin' in shoppin' malls?

What stifled his great grunts and groans
and got Cro-Magnon shaping stones?

Did the ol' lady beg for copper?
Who put that thought in her hopper?

Who messed with Mesopotamian minds
to get them counting sheep and hinds?

Who gave them so much to say
that they stamped thoughts into clay?

Who whispered in Egyptian ears
to make them top dogs all those years?

And how did they move eight ton blocks?
With palm tree logs? Rope and ox?

As if! Whoops, flop, bring the mop –
Who put the bop in the bop shu wop?

Folks just don't evolve that fast,
and who those days made things to last?

Like they were totally into Math
and ciphered each and every path –

Not! Where'd they get the technologies?
I'll tell you straight: from E.T.s!

The E.T.s used lasers to cut those stones,
and didn't do it to hide no bones!

They put the Ram in the ram-a-lam-a-ding-dong;
form-fitted the blocks, our genes, the whole she-bong!

Made Adam and Eve, the Garden, the Snake,
Mary, Jesus, and the whole clam bake!

Tiahuanaco, Stonehenge: the first computers
that turned us all into chic commuters.

They put the Bomp in the Bomp Ba Bomp,
gave us religion, the devil, the pomp;

put the dit in the dit, dit, dit, dit-da
that gave us cities, Wall Street, the Maidenform bra;

gave us the moon, the planets, the stars,
so we'd set our sights on Venus and Mars.

But what have we done with their retainers?
Shot the wad. Botched their "containers."

So now we're all Neanderthals
walkin' slack-jawed in shoppin' malls.

Lookin' for Mr. Goodwrench to keep us tight:
golems in Spandex, awaitin' our flight.

So come on, you saucer folk, sing us a song;
give us the ditty of Elephop 'n' ol' Elephong.

We've been waitin' too long to see God's face.
Drop the masks now; take us to space!

We're ready, baby; got tickets to punch!
Give us a call, and we'll do lunch!

The Mimicry Hypothesis

(to be read in a professional tone,
with Oxford accent)

The Mimicry Hypothesis,
though astonishing, is this:

Nimble E.T.s in disguise
have helped make mankind wise.

When we thought we saw the Virgin,
it was just a Grey emergin'.

To suddenly see E.T.s
might've given us D.T.s

To keep things light and airy,
they let us see a fairy;

and when we got into our selves,
they showed up as sprites and elves.

When our leaders were buffoons,
they let us see great big balloons.

Since we've emptied the bag 'n' tossed 'er,
they've shown up in flyin' saucers.

So if a statue should suddenly bleed,
don't go berserk and start a stampede,

and if her Nibs should then appear,
keep chin up; dispel your fear.

It's not some religious schtick;
it's just another E.T. trick!

How To Talk To An Extraterrestrial

No point in being abusive or rude –
unless you wanna be alien food.

Forget Urdu, Sanskrit, or Latin –
unless you want yer head to fatten.

English, Mandarin, or Cantonese
won't make 'em any weaker in the knees.

The Vulcan mind-melding technique
is about as useful as Hindi or Greek.

It's way too pushy and indiscreet,
as vacuous on our part as Lorikeet.

Chirp, chirp, chirp. What would we say?
They'd have our customs down in a day.

Ix-nay on Pig Latin or Val Speak too.
Esperanto'd get us a spot in a zoo.

Might as well grunt, walk on our knuckles,
use sign language or Smiles 'n' Chuckles.

No. Forget blatherin' in any tongue.
They'd as soon read entrails, examine our dung.

We're the furless monkeys here.
They're the egg heads; that is clear.

Best to listen, use mathematics.
Let our bats out of belfries and attics.

From one pencil-neck geek to the other,
swapping equations 'n' formulae one t'other –

that's the ticket! No pronunciation gaffs!
No giggles or sniggers, guffaws or laughs!

Geometry, Algebra, Calculus, Trig –
remember: their foreheads are really big!

You want to get inside their noodles,
you gotta put aside the Trix and Zoodles.

You can use spare change, loops and strings
to show them we know the planets and things.

Flash cards and flashlights are good too,
but pizza might make 'em gag or spew.

Pi – that's the new Rosetta stone
to get E.T.s to grab the phone.

Pi, as in p r^2, not lemon or flapper.
That'll reach alien scientist or kidnapper.

Quadratics will make 'em quake 'n' quiver
better than offerings of steak or liver.

Yeah. Pure math! Never mind what they are munchin'.
Let computer networks do the crunchin'!

Oannes

Oannes,
gentle merman, so myth says,
helped the men of Babylon
get on with building houses.

Gave men laws,
bade them bury teeth and claws,
seek out knowledge, truth and ways
to praise God, cope with their flaws.

Talked all day
about geometry and clay,
how to tell the seeds apart,
plant things in the heart and play.

Gave men Art,
and for his wisdom and part
in spinning this fine raiment,
took no payment, but took heart

that men might
build on this pillar of light
and put down their spears and knives,
build better lives, gain in sight.

Every day,
he gave them new words to say
love, trust, build, roots; showed them things
an alphabet brings from clay.

Descended
just before each day ended,
returned at dawn, to converse
and traverse ground he tended.

Thus did he
conspire with man to set free
their fettered minds, shape and bend
their dead-end course of enmity.

But, alas,
half-man, half-fish time did pass,
and raging tides claimed the land,
and Oannes became bass:

Fish to catch —
metaphor — mere hasp and latch
of words to tie a tale to,
and we too — slick and oil patch —

Up-ended:
spreading pools thought ammended,
reduced to greased molecules,
a cargo of thoughts intended.

Two Elders From Lemuria

Two elders from the land of Mu –
Lemurians perhaps –
or were they Nordic E.T.s
on sabbatical from the flaps?

Wandering up Mt. Shasta
lonely as two clouds,
with eyes as blue as Siamese cats'
and only sandals on their feet,
backpacks on their backs.

They weren't hitch-hiking hippies –
That I know is true,
but – oh – their eyes were beautiful
and -oh-so-liquid blue.

They looked at me; I looked at them,
and, grateful, they got in.
I drove them up the mountain then,
and, silent, they sat still.

Then, halfway up the mountain –
in the middle of this mist –
they whispered to me to stop
and became diaphanous.

Two Lemurians on the mountain.
Two monks in khaki togs.
Two whispers on the wind then
vanished in the fog.

Were they headed for lava caverns –
the last refuge after Mu –
or were they ghosts of legend –
Nordics on some mid-mountain rendezvous?

We slept the night in nylon
in a dome-shaped little tent,
but where the Lemurians had gone,
or what their passing meant,
was not a thought made clear.

A flash upon the mountain
in a blue beam beneath a craft
beamed up and had their tickets punched,
or else I'm going daft.

Two Lemurians on a mountain
became two winking stars.
Were they really new Venusians,
or did they come from Mars?
Two Lemurians on the mountain
soon winked out like two stars.

OINTs (Other Intelligences)

Well, you got us on your radar.
Yeah, you think you got a bite.
Gonna pay a little line out
and let us fuss and fight.

Gonna pay a little line out,
let us run with all our might.
Pay a little line out,
then drag us into sight.

But we ain't no cetacean, baby;
ain't no big fish on your line.
Your technology is ancient,
and you know we're feelin' fine.

You'll think you're reelin' us in
as we flash and splash,
then we'll leap out of the ocean
with style and panache.

Yeah, a porpoise with purpose,
we'll breach your frothy wake,
hit the sky in hyperdrive
and force you wide awake.

Cos we're OINTs in silver saucers
from the antediluvian sea.
Can't squeeze us into ointment –
Yeah, got no ambergris.

Your jets are just a joke, babe,
compared to our technology.
We're gonna mess with your magnetos.
Yeah, switch polarity.

Only one cat's got our number, babe.
You ain't payin' him no mind.
You think he's just a crackpot
and his thinking's so maligned.

He says we're other intelligences –
calls us OINTs for short –
and points to vile vortices
where time and space distort.

Yeah, ol' Ivan had it right, man:
we're an underwater clan.
Got no scales or flukes or flippers
cos we travel in a can.

We're an antediluvian species.
We live beneath the sea.
Bin on the earth forever –
before you were climbin' trees.

Got bases on other planets –
on Venus, Jupiter, and Mars.
Were warpin' in and out of worm holes
while you were building cars.

So now we scoot like Pac Men
across your radar screens,
and when you try to tag us,
we bag a few marines.

You get their last transmissions
of sighting UFOs,
but can't guess by gosh or golly
where their bones repose.

See, your boys may seem to vanish,
their planes plum disappear
when we gobble them like Pac Men
and turn space time on its ear.

But they're not nudgin' noses
with no friends of Davey Jones.
Their molecules are fine –
they've just crossed the line.

They may be discombobulated
from the weft and warp of time,
but they're hail and they're hearty;
their new genotypes are fine.

IV. BLACK HELICOPTERS

Area 51 (Dreamland)

Well, the Air Force brass deny it,
sunglass mantis eyes say no,
but way down in Nevada
there's a base the locals know.

There ain't no four-lane highway.
The perimeter's patrolled.
Signs are getting nasty
and the lies are getting old.

Area 51 they call it –
in the desert near Groom Lake.
Trespass, it's open season:
they'll skin you like a snake!

But high upon a ridge top
the boys with binos go
and every night they wait
for the flying saucer show.

Strange lights zip out this way,
strange lights zip out that.
Turn on a dime, oh-so-fine
like celestial acrobats.

They say no jet can match 'em;
the technology's not ours.
We've made a devil's bargain
with creatures from the stars.

They say they've got a saucer
with anti-gravity drive.
Aliens are teaching us
how to shuck and jive.

In return for anti-gravity
we've let them kill our cows.
They're making hybrid golems;
they're raising our high brows.

Yeah. Aliens are among us,
treat us like machines.
They're taking sperm and ova.
They're programming our genes!

Well, the Air Force brass deny it,
sunglass mantis yes say no,
but what's behind their glasses?
I'd really like to know.

High upon a ridge top
the boys with binos know,
and every night they wait
to catch the saucer show.

Black Helicopters

Above the backwoods of America!
Flyin' low over Manhattan!
Man, they're even up in Canada!
I tell you there's a patte'n!

Black choppers nabbing cattle!
Black choppers spraying gasses!
They're poisoning our livestock!
Chasing cars in mountain passes!

The Air Force doesn't own 'em.
The DEA won't lay no claim.
The FBI denies 'em.
They're coming just the same!

They're making guinea pigs of horses.
They're giving blackleg to our cows.
They're spreading evil viruses,
injecting mutigens in sows.

They're shooting passing motorists –
I tell you it's a crime!
They're protecting ET terrorists –
it happens all the time!

The government's made a bargain
with secret earth base greys.
They've been trading bovine plasma
for laser and death rays!

They're helping E.T.s abduct people,
so they can program all our genes!
Our DNA's mutating
before we hit our teens!

The government's in collusion!
We're dancing on puppet strings!
The E.T.s are making golems…
You gotta know these things!

There are no numbers on the choppers.
They swoop down in the night.
Snap you up and tag you
with some nasty parasite!

Aliens have got remote control,
program us through TV –
that night time glow's
a blue pseudopod, you see.

It envelopes us like an amoeba,
grabs our couch spud eyes.
They tell us what to consume;
we spread their "truth" like flies.

They're terra forming the planet, man!
Melting the polar caps!
Pretty soon we'll all have cancer
and be taking our dirt naps!

We gotta get those mantis mothers
outta those smoked glass domes,
nuke 'em where they hover, man!
Protect our property and homes!

We gotta clean house, route out
those traitorous E.T. Arnolds
and put 'em in our carnivals!
Get the sheep outta their folds!

Take control! Send those grey boys
packin' in their tea cups and saucers.
Yeah! We gonna clean up this planet, Janet!
It ain't no can! We can't just toss' er.

We gotta get on top of the situation, see.
Ain't no Tweedledum or Tweedledee
gonna be runnin' the show for no E.T.s!
We're gonna kick ass, get ourselves free!

Gonna blast them choppers outta the sky!
Gonna pull those Ray Ban specs
off those geek geezers in D.C.!
Gonna get those pencil necks –

Whoever the heck made this pact
with the E.T.s. We're gonna find
their underground bases and kick
their little skinny grey behinds!

Above the backwoods of America,
flyin' low over Manhattan …
Man, we're gonna kick yo' ass in Canada!
You won't know wha' happen'.

We're MIBS! *

We're MIBS — men in black suits
with black glasses and hats
black shoes and black pants
black shirts and black ties —
We're MIBS, we're MIBS, we're MIBS.

Don't you go tellin' no fibs.
You didn't see us; we were not here.
Our business-like look and demeanor
couldn't have got us away any cleaner.
We're MIBS, we're MIBS, we're MIBS.

We drive black Cadillacs and Mercedes
Are tall and thin, cadaverous and grim.
We carry clipboards, badges, and cards;
Arrive with black briefcases in tote.
We're MIBS, we're MIBS, we're MIBS.

Some say we're aliens come from the stars;
some say we're detectives, CIA spies —
spread disinformation, not lies.
You say you've seen saucers —
We say preposterous! We're MIBS.

We smile and cajole, take down your role
in these so-called alien abductions.
We say keep quiet, reveal thin wires
that peak from our cuffs and our shins.
We're MIBS, we're MIBS, we're MIBS.

Note: It's hard to represent all the dimensions of oral recitation of this one on the page. Imagine three characters in porkpie Stetsons and shades chanting the repetend lines together and taking turns interrupting each other to read the various lines of each stanza. Each caesura marks the pause that is the next speaker's cue. All the while the three are chanting, their movements are choreographed, so they march a few steps in each direction with briefcases in tote, coming together and changing directions on the beat.

We want information. A glass of water perhaps,
demographics and maps. Ask what you were doing
when the coffee was brewing, how many teeth
the cow had when it was chewing its cud.
We're MIBS, we're MIBS, we're MIBS.

We want to persuade you not to spread rumours,
lies and half-truths you say happened to you,
but are not so uncouth to suppose
anything more than a glimpse of a nose
will nip your own schnozzolas to size.
Oh no! We're MIBS; we're not of a violent kind.
We carry no brass knuckles or violin cases,
our credentials are most impeccable,
never mind that they cannot be traced.
We're MIBS, we're MIBS, we're MIBS.

We weren't here and you didn't see us.
The headaches will soon go away.
Your kids are beautiful, aren't they?
We'd like to see them grow up that way.
So don't go tellin' no fibs. No fibs. No fibs.

Camou Dudes Are Comin'!

(Area 51 Reprise)

Camou dudes are comin'!
You know I gotta run.
Camou dudes are comin'.
Gonna spoil all my fun.

Yeah, gotta stash my camera,
discombobulate my scopes.
Lam off with my lawn chair
before they dash my hopes.

Yeah, they'll confiscate my stuff,
slap cuffs on my po' wrists;
haul me to the hoosegow,
give this plot some twists!

They'll expose my black op shots,
destroy all the evidence
that I ever saw the saucers
or was ever near this fence.

You know they got these motion
'n' ammonia sensors here.
They can track a skeeter's buzz,
even measure drops of fear!

They call this place "the box";
won't let the fly boys in.
If they stray into this air space,
they lose their stripes and skin!

Yeah. These camou dudes are touchy.
Like to fidget with their toys.
They'd as soon shoot as greet you.
You don't wanna meet those boys.

They call this place "The Ranch."
It ain't on no survey maps –
ain't got no edges either –
lots of room for long dirt naps.

The camou dudes got jeeps,
quiet black op choppers too!
They can swoop right out of nowhere.
Then what chew gonna do?

They don't like no interlopers.
Gonna dis this Freedom Ridge.
Grab you off yo' skinny pegs
and stick you in some fridge.

So you best be watchin', baby –
and I don't just mean the skies.
Saucer photos sell to tabloids,
but so would our hushabyes.

Ain't no time to sit and rap, son,
when the camou dudes are creepin'.
I don't like to wake up dead, you see –
my bed is where I'm sleepin'.

Yeah! Camou dudes are comin'
in camouflage fatigues.
Listen! Cicadas won't say nada,
even if you start intrigues.

You wanna catch the final platter
outta this skeet shootin' rig,
put a quarter in the juke box, baby,
cos that's how you make this gig.

Push "Flyin' Saucer Rock 'n' Roll,"
not some deep six lullaby.
Watch the moon come up for change
and spin another sequined sky.

Tomorrow we'll bring cameras,
ignore the discouraging words;
dream of strange attractors
and lunar ungulent herds.

We'll roast our weenies safely,
play blues harp to the stars.
Yodel to Wile E. Coyote
and stick closer to our cars!

Mobile Blood Bank Withdrawal

West Virginia, it seems,
has had its share of saucer flaps.
Meandering lights, u.f.o.s,
weird phone calls, bleeps, and taps.

Lovers parked in lovers lanes
zapped with actinic rays
wake to wicked sun burns
that betray their buff soirees.

Orange lights over backyards
respond to flashlight code
with knock knock 'lectronic blips
in shave-and-haircut mode.

Some E.T.s have their fun with us,
answer every tit with tat.
Others expect us to cry "Uncle"
when they pin us to the mat.

MIBs were making housecalls
too weird to call a hoax
while the TNT site Mothman
scared the bejesus out of folks.

But the creepiest critters of all –
'cept werewolves and poltergeists –
were the badass saucer vampires
who nearly pulled off the blood bank heist.

No guff! A mobile blood truck
had just finished a donor run,
was flush with hemoglobin
at the setting of the sun.

Was traveling along Route 2,
bound for Huntington that night,
when suddenly above the treeline
the driver saw a brilliant light.

It was like a star was trailing them –
as weird as all get out –
The nurse wound down her window
and let go this wicked shout!

The light was no satellite or star,
but a saucer directly overhead!
It was jockeying into position
with heavy metal pinchers spread!

The driver put pedal to the metal,
but the crazy crabboid craft
matched them turn for turn,
and our driver would be daft

were it not for a stroke of luck:
car lights appeared over the rise,
made our saucer vampires retract
their pinchers and head for the skies.

"Saucer vampires indeed!" you scoff,
but I swear every detail here is true!
E.T.s want our blood. They use it
to make hybrids that look like me and you!

They've got bigger foreheads and weird eyes –
pass in stetsons and sunglasses though.
Pose as cops on lonely highways,
stop motorists with their heighdy-ho.

If you pull over, they've got you cold.
One look in those eyes, you're hypnotized!
The next thing you don't know
you're inspected – grade A – compromised!

They've got you on some saucer gurney,
scrape your skin, poke and pry,
float you back down behind the wheel,
so you're lookin' at yer watch, wondering why

you ain't home yet. How come two hours
have somehow suddenly disappeared?
You've got scoop marks, headache,
wicked warts and rash, and you feel weird.

You don't know why every time
you hear a buzz or the phone rings
a weird crackling or metallic voice
has got you doing unusual things.

You get in your car, go to the store,
drive off on some lonely back road
for God-only-knows what reason.
Then see where they've got their saucer stowed.

Oh yeah! You know then, but you'll forget!
They've tagged you like some slo-eyed deer;
you'll go about your business – and theirs too!
and do their bidding year after year.

Maybe next time you think you're working
for the Red Cross on some altruistic mission,
they'll make a withdrawal, wreck your van,
leave you wishin' you didn't want to go fishin'!

But that's the way it is, my friend.
Once you're tagged, you're stuffed and bagged!
May as well mount yourself on a wall
as wait for the next time you're flagged!

The Strange Death of Philip Schneider

Philip Schneider was a good guy,
a patriot and friend.
He could not abide the lies;
he came to a bad end.

He knew all about explosives –
was a structural engineer.
He was in on black op contracts
and secrets we don't fear.

One day while making tunnels
beneath the Dulce desert sands,
proof of Air Force - grey collusion
fell right into his hands.

He thought he was helping build
an underground Air Force base
when a planned detonation
opened up a hollow space.

It was no secret vault
or old mine shaft that he'd found,
but a secret E.T. base
built miles underground.

He came face to face with aliens
and high-ranking Air Force brass.
He couldn't keep that secret,
and they wouldn't let it pass.

Oh yeah. He clearly saw the enemy:
the enemy was us!
It was like staring down a laser
with a rusty blunderbuss.

He was one of three survivors
to live to tell the tale,
but felt like poor ol' Jonah
living life inside a whale.

He'd learned horrible secrets
about the fate of all mankind,
but no one in the media
would pay him any mind.

They thought he was a whacko –
some sasquatch - E.T. buff;
he was talking crazy nonsense
and sleazy tabloid fluff.

He told us our own government
was building prison railway cars,
that aliens had built bases
on the earth, the moon, and Mars.

He said we'd signed a treaty
way back in fifty-four;
had approved of bovine mutilations
and abductions by the score.

We'd given the greys an inch;
now they're taking every mile.
A secret world order exists –
and assists the greys in style!

Black helicopters with computers
can see us move from room to room,
will fill the skies like locusts,
and every grain of truth consume.

Sixty-eight percent of spending
on U.S. military might
is black budget allocated,
whisked clean out of our sight.

Even the Space Defense Initiative –
Ronnie Ray Gun's Star Wars plan –
was never really built
to stop us from killing man.

No. Star Wars, laser, HAARP,
Stealth, fibre optics, chips –
all back-engineered technologies –
were taken from space ships.

Armageddon, when it gets here,
won't destroy the human race,
but some mutant hybrid species
that's already taking our place!

Ol' Phil may have been a little nuts —
he had his mental trials –
but when they got into his fortress,
they killed him and stole his files.

They made it look like suicide,
just like he'd said they would.
Now there are only two of us,
but I wouldn't tell you if I could.

No. There's a buzzin' in my head
that sounds like a dial tone,
and every time I talk aloud
it's like there ain't nobody home.

Huh?

If light can be a particle,
and light can be a wave,
couldn't UFOs be objects
that sometimes misbehave?

If there really is no future,
and there really is no past,
could not the present also
be a time that doesn't last?

Could time then be elastic
as objects are in space?
A UFO be sitting here
and be some other place?

Could the eye just be a vortex
into which an object falls?
And time be just an ant
or the sand on which it crawls?

Could UFOs be time machines?
E.T.s be humankind?
Or are they projected holograms,
a trick of light or mind?

Could a man's white hair be snow
on some high-peaked roof?
Is this now the answer
or some future proof?

Element 115

Bob Lazar says we've got 'em –
nine saucers at Groom Lake alone!
Some like tops, some like plates,
one like an acorn or pine cone.

They're powered by a heavy metal
they call element one-fifteen.
Use an anti-gravity device
to create their anti-gravity.

I dunno, but I've been told
ridin' a reactor's kinda bold.
A guy might end up with unzipped genes,
and I don't dig those party scenes.

Let the E.T.s split new isotopes;
I'd as soon slice cantaloupes.

SWAG (Sophisticated Wild-Ass Guess)

So what's the skinny on these little grey guys?
Are they really leprechauns in disguise?
Extraterrestrial saucer folk –
or some guy's idea of a bad joke?

Are they time sliders flyin' in hyperdrive?
Insectoid workers from an outer space hive?
Or hallucinations from some brain lesion
that don't speak English, French, or Frisian?

Are they interstellar space invaders?
Or golems in spandex and hip waders?
Are they fairies, sprites, trolls, or elves
who wear lamé leotards off the shelves?

And what's their intergalactic mission,
if not to nab us when we're fishin'?
Are they the tailors who stitched our genes,
or some kinda flesh-and-blood machines?

And, if flesh-and-blood, then how the heck
do they walk through walls so circumspect?
Are they ghosts, phantoms, or holograms?
How much do they weigh, in kilograms?

Are they angels of mercy minus the wings,
or demons doing dastardly deeds and things?
Are they silent succubi flying in saucers,
ancient incubi, or pencil-neck tossers?

Are they pasty-faced computer geeks
who've stayed indoors for weeks and weeks,
or ninety-pound weaklings who never enrolled
in weight training or Judo or even bowled?

How much RAM do their crania contain
with no slots for follicles, such a big brain?
How do they carry such melons at all
with such skinny necks and muscles so small?

How did they get here, and how procreate
with no navels or genitals or hips to gyrate?
Do they have normal humanoid relations
or android conniptions, sympathetic vibrations?

Who would hazard a SWAG with these scalawags?
They've got no ID, SIN, VISA or vehicle tags.
They ain't from Kansas, Oz, or Timbuktu.
What's a peace officer here supposed to do?

They refuse to land on the White House lawn.
We can't kick their tires. They string us along.
Worm through wormholes, then disappear,
yet keep comin' back, year after year.

They hypnotize and stare at us with mantis eyes,
levitate, read our minds, de- and re-materialize;
are telepathic, control traffic, capable of many things
that make us dance like puppets on their strings.

With such quirks and dumb shows in the works,
the way each string sometimes sways, sometimes jerks,
you gotta wonder if God is just a virus too –
an alien implant: inoculation for me and you.

Not a greybeard controlling wheels and levers –
anthropomorphic WASP or eager beaver –
but a great deep black hole of an oversoul
toward which we're moving by remote control.

The Wanderer

(to the tune by Ernie Maresca)

Oh well, I'm the type of guy
that can never settle down.
Ain't from these grey meninges,
let alone this Hicksville town.

They punch my star flight ticket
when you slap a baby's bum.
I enter through her wail – O –
'fore she plugs it with her thumb.

Cos I'm a wanderer.
Oh, yeah, a wanderer.
I roam around, around,
roam from town to town.

Got a soul transfer from out there.
Yeah, I'm a real gone cat!
Come from the Pleides.
Babe, you know that's where it's at!

I fit snug into your cranium,
a bug that cuts a rug.
I'm a cold cut in your Tupperware,
a refrigerated bug.

Cos I'm a wanderer.
Oh, yeah, a wanderer.
I roam around, around,
roam from star to star.

I live inside your brain, babe,
a sweet-talkin' viral guy.
You're the hostess with the mostes';
I'm a pill with tux 'n' tie.

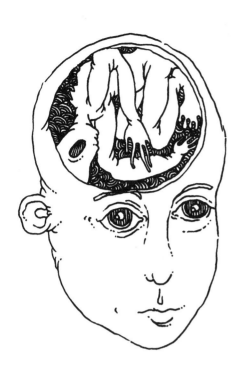

I live a life of leisure,
cruise your satin sheets.
I'm your soulful soul mate sister,
your mister twister spirochete.

Cos I'm a wanderer.
Oh yeah, a wanderer.
I roam around, around,
ain't sayin' where I'm bound.

I'm the cream in your coffee,
crookcd top to crookcd pot.
I steep inside you, baby;
am your will and only thought.

I'm here to raise your consciousness,
create a rock 'n' roll bee hive,
so when the saucers get here
your folks can shuck 'n' jive.

Cos I'm a wanderer.
Oh, yeah, a wanderer.
I buzz around, around,
flit from dome to dome.

Cos I'm a wanderer.
Oh, yeah, a wanderer.
Your very own Dick Tater
playin' in your pia mater

Cos I'm a wanderer.
Oh, yeah, a wanderer.

(fade)

Walk-in Blues

Well, I'm a walk-in
Venusian blues man,
a walkin', talkin'
Venusian/ hu-man.

Got me a homo s. chassie –
a sassy planet earth lassie.
I'm lean and I'm mean
and I'm classy.

You don't know it
whenever you pass me.
Think I'm way too sexy
to ask me –

my headlights just blind
your foggy homo s. mind
to the truth of my
kith or my kind.

Ain't Ms. Frankenstein
or anyone's bride.
My mind is all mine,
is working just fine.

I should float through my day
the celestial way,
never mind moats
or the hassle of castles.

Don't need
no princess phone
or room of my own,
let alone the stuff you all own.

I should float down the aisle,
not walk mile after mile
from diapers to dresses,
shampoo for these tresses,

but I occupy
the most stygian sty
of grey matter
and azure blue sky:

somehow got inside
just as her majesty died,
the good doc revived
her fine alabaster hide.

So now I'm in the pink
with my hands in the sink:
a walk-in D.P.
who pulled this K.P.

I'm a walk-in
Venusian blues man –
so terribly, terribly
hu-man.

I need a shrink
to help me un-think,
unplug this grey sink,
get me in sync.

I'm a human-
lookin' Venusian
sufferin' some
wicked contusion,

a walk-in
Venusian blues man,
a walkin', talkin'
Venusian/hu-man.

I need to get
out of this hide,
change genders besides.
O, woe betide

this lovely host hide
that's got me uptight.
I'm sure she was nice
even cool blue on ice.

But who's gonna die twice?
That wouldn't be nice.
Even poor Heidi Fleiss
couldn't broker the price.

So I go through my days
walkin' fashion runways,
let dumb men appraise
the tinsel and glaze

while they gawk agog,
their brains in a fog
and I set the pace
in my blonde carapace,

share some finer illusions
in this bod that I'm usin'
with a car crash victim
whose heart kept on tickin',

and, you know, she's O.K.
had much more to say
than these silly dorks
who watch the hams she desports.

So I'm doubly confused,
twice gladly removed
from this sordid play
that has me walkin' all day.

I'm wiser but saddened
by what I see hadn't
happened to this
beautiful young miss

who chose aloofness
over slaverin' doofness,
and I'm a sorry
Venusian whose glory

got parked by the curb
with her husband, Herb.
I'm a confused hu-man/
Venusian blues man.

Wanna whack his poor pod
insteada shakin' this bod,
but will walk off the stage
one day in a rage

and will get a new life –
and, yeah, maybe a wife –
so I can play
the masculine fool.

Yeah, I'm a walk- in
Venusian blues man,
so terribly
warily hu-man.

Gonna park Herb by the curb,
take a sudden curve
with élan and cool verve,
gonna walk my po' blues away.

Yeah, gonna walk
and talk and chew gum,
say, Bub, kiss my bum.
I'm outta here, Chum!

I'm a walk-in
Venusian blues man,
a walk-in, talkin'
Venusian/hu-man.

Gonna take what consciousness
didn't set in the west;
gonna move this po' chassie,
this homo s lassie

to new heights of hu-man/
Venusian blueness.
Gonna replace the vacancy sign
with an occupied mind.

Yeah, I might have to stay,
just so she'll get her way
cos I'm terribly terribly hu-man,
a hu-man/Venusian blues man.

A hu-man/Venusian blues man…
A hu-man/Venusian blues man …

(fade)

Ultraterrestrial Ultimatum

The thing about us saucer folk
most humans fail to see
is that we've always been among you,
though our ways are slippery.

The E.T. hypothesis is fun, of course,
has us flitting from earth to stars,
and, yes, we have the technology,
but, no, we're not from Mars.

We don't travel from other galaxies,
let alone some distant place;
we simply transmogrify reality,
mess with time and space.

Just as dogs can hear high frequencies
that most humans cannot hear,
we are attuned to other dimensions
than the three through which you steer.

When we travel to the edge of infrared,
or the ultraviolet of human range,
we boot it into hyperdrive
and our molecules go strange.

To you it seems we disappear
right off your radar screens.
We're there one second, gone the next;
blow your jets to smithereens!

But we're really not so violent;
don't so much blow folks away
as re-arrange their molecules,
the sandbox in which they play.

We take 'em through a wormhole
to a universe next door,
let them cruise in astral bodies
and explore the heretofore.

True, they can't manifest themselves
in your spectrum like we can,
but they're happy and collected,
not spam served au gratin.

Likewise with yer crypto critters –
The Loch Ness Monster and Bigfoot –
You can't ever nab or bag 'em
cos their molecules don't stay put.

We materialize and de-materialize
kangaroos, big cats, entire herds
of burger cattle. They look bemused,
look for food, leave scat and turds

that have you scratchin' yer noodles,
checkin' for vacancies in zoos,
and, sometimes, you blame the viewer,
put sightings down to drugs or booze.

It amuses us to watch you bag
scat and fur, take plaster casts
to speculate and catalogue
all the "evidence" you've amassed.

Really! We're just sub-letting space and time
for extinct and endangered species,
providing interdimensional eco-niches,
so to speak. We don't weigh their feces!

As far as that goes, it's you humans
that sputter and spew, exude
the most methane and poo. It's you
who pollute, extract, and extrude.

You aren't content with polluting this planet;
you gotta flush the atmosphere!
Pardon us for letting loose
the occasional Bronx cheer!

We're impish and devious beings
because we have to be, you see.
You call your toilets thrones
and crap on eternity!

Hold the phone there homo s.!
You'll be most enlightened to know
you're not alone! Big surprise!
You're not even runnin' the show!

Extra! Extra! We're not Martian mutants,
fairies, trolls, leprechauns, or E.T.s!
We're ultra—not extra-terrestrials!
Time to genuflect, get down on your knees!

We're bendin' your reality, baby!
So wrap your brain around this:
we're gonna change your D.N.A., honey!
Ain't gonna put up with no homo s. dis!

Mary, Mary… Not So Contrary

If Mary was a virgin,
'n' Joseph wasn't Jesus' Dad,
how could Mary have a baby,
let alone a strapping lad?

Parthenogenesis is one way –
the way of certain frogs
who larrup and get listless
when stood up in their bogs.

But Mary wasn't lonely
and Joe was a handy man.
It's not like he was absent
or rotting in some can.

Joseph was a model parent,
a brilliant family planner;
a spark certainly ignited,
and he was there to fan 'er.

But, O.K., let's say God
was Johnny on the spot.
Joseph was away that day.
Things went from warm to hot.

The holy ghost got down –
in a metaphysical way –
an immaculate breeze
got past her knees, let's say.

Would it be so blasphemous then
to suggest God did not intervene
in some unspoken plot,
some wholly other scene?

The North Star that shone so bright –
could it have been a U.F.O.?
Could Mary have been abducted
and missed part of the blesséd show?

If she were artificially inseminated
with better-than-human seed,
would that mean God had done
some sordid or nefarious deed?

Would Jesus, the son, then be
any less a son of God
with a twin complement of genes –
half-human, half alien demigod?

Does it matter whether the curtain
is parted, or partially closed;
that we see God's face for a moment
an all-too-human thought is exposed?

Would it make any difference
to a man's faith in the divine
if he got a glimpse of his roots
as well as the leaf and vine?